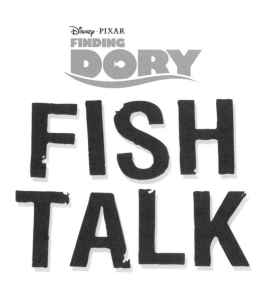

FISH TALK

Oh, hello! Didn't
see you there.

DISNEY · PIXAR
FINDING
DORY

FISH TALK

By Suzanne Francis

Illustrated by Premise Entertainment

DISNEP PRESS

Los Angeles • New York

CHARACTERS

DORY

MARLIN and **NEMO**

HANK

FLUKE and **RUDDER**
(and GERALD)

BECKY

DESTINY and **BAILEY**

STARFISH

BURROWING CUCUMBER

ANEMONE

SEA WORM

LOUDMOUTH CLAM

BILL and **CAROL**

JENNY and **CHARLIE**

BLUE TANGS 1, 2, and 3

OFFICER DAVE

LITTLE DORY

DEEP IN THE OCEAN
(Some time ago)

Hi. I'm **Dory**.

Do you know where I live? Maybe you saw which way I came from? I don't know what happened.

Oh. I'm Dory, by the way.

I suffer from short-term memory loss, so I can't remember sometimes.

I lost my parents and I've been searching for them and asking anyone who will listen, but . . . no one has been able to help.

Can you? No? That's okay.

Oh, hi, there! I'm losty . . . I mean, Dory. *Whew* . . . It's really quiet down here, isn't it? I haven't seen anyone else in a while. I'm kind of wondering if anyone can help me.

Hellooo? Can you hear me now? I gotta say, it's a little scary. . . .

Okay. Um. What can I do, what can I do?

Just keep swimming, swimming, swimming. . . .

And singing . . . Yes!

Sing a song about . . . something not scary.
Like . . . spaghetti!

> Oh, spag-hetti spagheeeeetti—
> you're delicious and fun.
> Like confeeeeetti.
> I love you a ton!
> And you're never scary.
> You're always there-y . . .
> for meeeee.
> I think you must be
> my des-ti-nyyyyy!

Oh. Hi. Did you happen to see which way
I came from? Maybe you know where my
parents are? I'm lost. And I really miss them.

Did you see which way I came from? I can't
remember because I suffer from short-term
memory loss.

You hear that? That growly rumbling noise.

Was it a
WHAAAaaaaaLLLLLe?

Hmmm . . . must get bad reception out here. Was it my stomach? I *am* kind of hungry.

Oooh, do you have a churro? Because I love churros and I would definitely say yes if you offered one. Wait. Was I the one in charge of the churro? If I was, I think I ate it.

You know, sometimes I feel like I'm looking for something . . . but I can't remember what it was. . . . See, I suffer from short-term memory loss, so it happens a lot.

Ooooh! Is that a sparkling jewel? Was that what I was looking for?

Oh, no. Shiny piece of seaweed.

Bummer. It's kind of pretty, though.

I like shiny things. I wonder if I was supposed
to find a shiny thing?

Oh. My name's Dory, by the way.
I'm pretty sure I lost something. I just can't
remember what it was. . . .

A **wrench** . . .

or something
squishy?

Was it
shells?

I *love* shells! I think I'm supposed to remember something about shells. I hope it wasn't important. Well, I'm sure I'll know it when I find it. I'll just keep swimming.

MARLIN (Ⓜ) and NEMO (Ⓝ)

GREAT BARRIER REEF
(Present Day)

Ⓜ I'm a clownfish.

And no, that doesn't mean I'm full of jokes and hilarious one-liners. That's a common misconception about clownfish. I'm not really very funny at all.

Ⓝ I think you're funny, Dad.

M Thanks, Son. Oh. This is my son, Nemo.

N Hi.

M We live here on the reef. It's a great area. Beautiful views. Safe. Family-friendly. Nemo goes to school and loves it. His teacher, Mr. Ray, is the best.

N Yeah, I love Mr. Ray. And Dory comes to school with me, too, sometimes. She helps Mr. Ray with the class.

M Yeah. "Helps." We keep an eye on Dory. She needs a little extra guidance—reminders and things, you know.

N I try and remind her about the anemone. She forgets that a lot. I think she's probably been stung a hundred times!

M Yup . . . Dory and I traveled across the ocean together to save my son.

The only reason I did something so crazy was that I was looking for Nemo.

Nothing is more important to me than family, and without Nemo . . . well, let's just say it was worth fighting the four giant sharks for him. It would have been worth fighting four hundred!

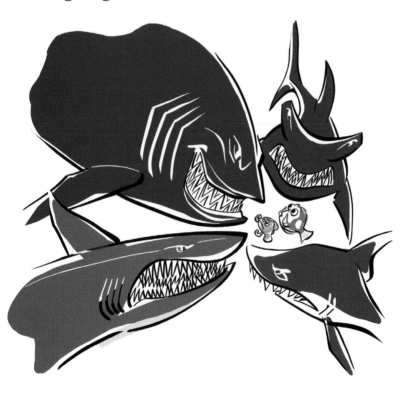

N Four? I thought you said it was three sharks.

M No, no, Nemo. It was definitely four. And they were big. With lots of teeth. I should know–I was there.

N You said three last time you told it, Dad.

M Well, three or four or four hundred . . . What matters most is that we made it home, safe and sound back on the reef.

N Being home is great, but traveling is also fun—

M Being home *is* great and traveling is only fun after you get home.

N But that's why we have to help Dory. She wants to get back to her home. Back to where she's from. It's just like what we learned about at school. Migration is nature's way—

M Yes, I know. And we are going to help Dory. I just wish we didn't have to go so far.

N We're going all the way to California. Because that's where she's from! See, today Mr. Ray took us on a field trip to watch the stingrays migrate, and Dory came along. It was incredible! But Dory blacked out. She just fell over with her eyes closed, like this.

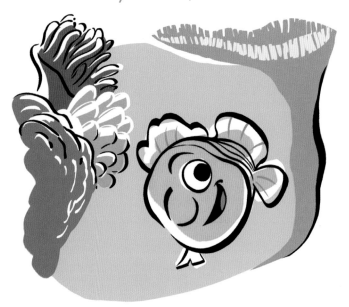

And she was murmuring, "The Jewel of Morro Bay, California." It was crazy! Then, when she woke up, she remembered something, but she couldn't remember what she remembered.

M That pretty much sums up Dory.

N But when I told her that she was saying, "The Jewel of Morro Bay, California," she remembered again! She remembered her parents! I think this whole thing is nature's way of getting Dory back home—of getting her to *migrate*.

M You're sure she didn't say, "The Jewel of Brisbane Bay, *Australia*," right? 'Cause that would be a whole lot–

N Dad, for the first time in her life . . . Dory remembered. It's got to be right.

M I know. But we are talking about a fish who thinks she can communicate with whales and does the robot in her sleep.

N I love when she does that!
Bneep-bnorp-nop-nop. (Laughs)

M Annnnnd we're letting the "whale-speaking robot" book our travel.

N We're not just traveling. We're helping her migrate and get back home! It's really important.

M I know, Nemo. I know how important family is and that is why we're going to help Dory. We have to go. You know I would never be able to stay here while Dory went across the ocean all by herself.

N Yes! We're off to have another adventure!

I can't wait!

Let's go!

DORY

EN ROUTE TO
The Jewel of Morro Bay, California

I REMEMBERED SOMETHING!

Can you believe it?
I remembered my parents!

It's not totally clear who they are or what they look like, but I think they might look

something like **this**.

Or maybe it was **this**.

Or **this**?

Is anyone else craving churros right now?

Anyway, it doesn't matter, because thanks to Nemo—he helped me—I remembered what I had remembered!

Wait—what were we talking about? Your parents? Oh, right, *my* parents! My *family*! They're in some sort of pearl of something in California, and Marlin and Nemo are going to help me find them!

Which is great, because I'm not so good on my own, you know? I'd never make it without them. See, I forget things and so . . . it's hard for me to get anywhere by myself.

Guess what—we're on our way across the ocean to find my family at the gem of Calistoga . . . or something!

Oooh, I'm so excited I can't wait! I just have to make sure we don't get separa—

Whoops.

It seems I have gotten lost. By myself. This
can't be good.

Hey—what are these shiny round things?
Wait a minute. Where am I?

Hello, do you know the way to the jewel of
Cambodia? No . . . that's not right. Where am
I going again? Zorro's Cape? No, that wasn't
it. Morro Bay!

Whoa! Wait!

Ahhhhh!

Let go! Where are you taking me?
I don't wanna go in there! Oh, no. Marlin and
Nemo will come get me. They'll come get
me—

HANK

QUARANTINE
Marine Life Institute, Morro Bay, California

Wasn't born that way, and no, I won't tell you the story.
Go ahead. Take a look.

8 = OCTOPUS

Count 'em up. One, two, three, four, five, six, seven. There ya go. Yup. I'm a septopus, not an octopus. Get over it. I have.

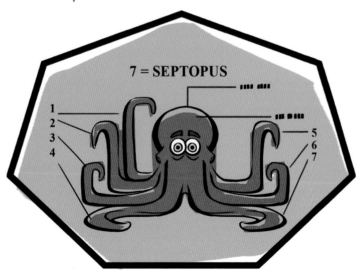

7 = SEPTOPUS

So I've been here at the Marine Life Institute for a while and I can't wait to get outta this joint. Not that there's anything wrong with actually being in the institute. MLI is fine.

The staffers are clueless enough that I can get around and do my thing, which I like. Sure, they're always looking for me and that's annoying, but I've gotten pretty good at hiding in plain sight. No one ever notices me when I'm disguised as a lamp, for example.

And just this morning there was a staffer right in front of me in the supply closet. I thought he was gonna bag me for sure, but I blended into a value pack of toilet paper. He was clueless!

Camouflage is a handy talent to have, that's for sure.

Anyway, the problem with the institute is this: you don't stay forever. All roads lead to one of two places—the ocean or Cleveland. And I am not going back to the ocean. That place is one big hassle.

First of all, unless you're at the top of the food chain—which I ain't—it's basically a giant pit of death.

Another thing: it's a very gossipy place. Everyone gets into everyone's business. I've been looking for peace and quiet for about as long as I can remember. Big family.

And by "big," I mean loud, obnoxious, and annoying. Always in my face about something. A bunch of nonsense.

If I get to Cleveland, it'll be permanent digs

in an aquarium. Free room and board in the safety of a tank for the rest of my life . . . Now that's what I'm talking about.

And as luck would have it, as I was sneaking around Quarantine today I met this kooky blue tang fish with a transport tag. That's the ticket. Everyone with a tag gets put on the truck and sent to Cleveland. You follow me? If I get a tag, I get on the truck.

So I made a deal with the nut fish. Her name's Dory, by the way. She's looking for her family. Not sure why anyone would wanna do that, but anyway . . . If I help her, she hands over the tag. Done deal.

Funny thing about Dory, though—she's got some oddball memory issue, so she forgets things. To tell you the truth, I wouldn't mind a little case of that myself. I've had plenty of experiences I'd like to forget. Seems to me no memories, no problems.

Anyway, because of her memory thing, she repeats herself. A lot. She's always talking, asking a bunch of questions—and yeah, it's irritating. I don't do well with chatty. Not to mention the fact that she's oozing with bright, shiny positivity.

You know the type? "There's always a way!" That "Rah! Rah! Never give up" and "Everything will work out" sort of baloney. But . . . you know what? I can take it. It'll all be worth it once I'm in Cleveland.

Ahhh, Cleveland . . . I'll be smelling the sweet fumes of a truck bound there by morning. For now I just have to get through helping that wacky little blue tang find her folks. It turns out she's from this place—MLI, aka The Jewel of Morro Bay, California. Should be easy enough.

FLUKE (F) and RUDDER (R) (and GERALD (G))

CLUSTER OF ROCKS
Morro Bay, outside Marine Life Institute

Nothing beats a nice warm **rock**, hey, mate?

Yeah. Rock feels **extra nice** today.

(Giggles)

F Yeah. (Yawn)

R (Yawn)

F Yeah. (Yawn)

R (Yawn)

F Best rock in the ocean, it is.

R Ain't it, though? (Yawn)

F I'm feeling a little hungry. You?

R Eh. Sure, yeah. I'd eat a fish if there was one in front of me.

F Rock service, that's what we need.

R Lovely idea, mate. Order me up a chubby one. (Laughs)

F (Laughs) Yeah, nice and fat. Not like those little clownfish we met today.

R Niblets, they were.

F Though I would have snacked on them had they been a little closer.

R Oh, yeah. Course. (Yawn)

F Had to feel for 'em a bit, though. Losing their friend inside the institute and all.

R Yeah. But there are worse places to be lost.

F True, true.

R The free meals were nice.

F Good point, mate. Not worth getting another nasal parasite, though. Nasty bout, that was.

R (Laughs) Terrible. Not worth the anemia, either. Made me feel so tired all the time. (Yawn)

F Yeah. Can't have that. (Yawn)

G (Giggles)

R Is that Gerald? Better not be!

G (Giggles)

R Gerald! What do you think you're—

G (Barks)

F Shove off, Gerald! This is our rock! (Barks) Off! Off! Off!

R Oy! (Barks) Get off the rock, Gerald!

F Get off the rock! Outta here, Gerald!

R OFF YA GO, GERALD!

F The nerve.

R He's got it, all right.

F (Yawn) Shivvy over a tad bit, will ya, mate?

R Sure, sure.

F (Grunts)

R (Grunts)

F Ahhh. Even better.

R Oh, yeah. (Yawn)

F Wonder how those little clownfish are doing. Our good deed for the year, right, mate?

R Yeah, that was quite nice of us, helping them along, telling them their friend would be taken to Quarantine straightaway, having Becky take them there and all. They'll be safe and sound under her wing and in Gerald's little pail full of water, right?

F That's right. Loon Airways. (Laughs)

I wonder if they made it to Quarantine yet. . . . Good chance of it. As long as Captain Becky didn't get hungry. (Laughs)

R (Laughs) She does have an appetite on her, don't she?

F And she ain't afraid to work for it, either. Makes me tired just thinking about it. (Yawn) I'm drifting off, mate. I'll see you in a few.

R Yeah . . . me too. Melting right into this rock. Like magic, it is.

F Best rock in the world.

R Don't even think about it, Gerald.

BECKY

EN ROUTE TO QUARANTINE
Air above Marine Life Institute

Squawk!
Squawk!
Squawk!

Cooo-ooooo-ooooo. Oo-roooo. Oooo-rooo
cooo-ooooo-ooooo. Oo-roooo. Oooo-rooo
loooo.

Cooo-ooooo-ooooo. Oo-roooo. Oooo-rooo.

Oo-roooo. Oooo-rooo oo-roooo.

Oooo-rooo. Oo-roooo. Oooo-rooo.

Looo-looo.

Cooo-ooooo-ooooo. Oo-roooo.

Oooo-rooo oooo-roooo. Oooo-rooo

oo-roooo. Oooo-rooo.

Squawk! Squawk! Squawk!

Looo loo loo loo.

Oo-roooo. Oooo-rooo oo-roooo.

Oooo-rooo. Cooo-ooooo-ooooo.

Oo-roooo. Oooo-rooo.

Cooo-ooooo-ooooo. Oo-roooo.

Oooo-rooo. Looo. Loo loo loo.

Loo looo loo loo.

Oo-roooo. Oooo-rooo.

Cooo-ooooo-ooooo.

Oo-roooo. Oooo-rooo.

Cooo-ooooo-ooooo.

Oo-roooo. Oooo-rooo.

Editor's translation:

As the loon flies toward the west,
She doth what she doth best.
Flapping, soaring, flapping loon,
Take the pail of clownfish.
Fly with the moon.

Take your precious cargo.
Fly to the tune
Of your lonely heartbeat,
Beating in your lonely
Loon-ey
Chest.

Oh! *What's this?*
Oh, could it be?
Do my eyes see what they see?

What glory has fallen on this fine day?
Drops of golden beauty . . .
Ye take my breath away!

Puffy little clouds of corn,
You do make this loon's heart soar.

Orange friends, wait in your pail.
Puff corn is the Holy Grail.

At this moment, I do yearn.
Fear not, little fish, I shall return!

DORY

CHUM BUCKET
Marine Life Institute

Okay, I'm actually here. **I'm here!**

Evidently, *this* place is the drool of Torro Bay in California—the place where my parents are! Do you believe it? Now I just have to find them. . . .

And what's really crazy is that, in a way, it feels sorta familiar here. Like I dreamed about it or . . . like I've been here before—I guess because I have! I am *from* here, so that means I have been here before.

Boy, these guys don't look too good, huh? I don't know how they do that for so long. Hello? Are you okay? Not a talker in the bunch, huh? Oh, well. It's okay. You guys rest. I'm good.

Anyway, I met this grouchy septopus. He has seven tentacles so he's a septopus, not an octopus. Could be why he's so grouchy. His name's Frank or . . . Phillip . . . Felix . . . something like that.

Anyway, he said he'd help me find my parents, so he was taking me around. I actually think he's secretly sort of sweet even though he complains a lot and makes this really serious grumpy face all the time.

But it felt like destiny. You know, that we met. Like it was meant to be. Then I saw this bucket. And do you see what the bucket says?

DESTINY!

So I had to jump in with these guys—right, guys? Hello? Still nothing, huh?—because I just knew that I should. . . .

I'm sure Franco will just meet us wherever we end up. No, that wasn't his name. Was it Rico? No. Anyone? You guys know? Have you seen a septopus around? No? Not looking too good, guys. Oh, I get it! You're playing dead. Good idea!

Well, I'm not sure where I'm off to now, but I'm getting closer to finding my parents. I can feel it!

DESTINY (**D**) and BAILEY (**B**)

WHALE TANK
Marine Life Institute

Dory?
I know Dory!

Oh, my
head.

D It's crazy. Dory and I were really good friends.
I know it's weird that we had never even met
face to face until today, but we were really
close when we were little. We talked all the
time. We were pipe pals.

She lived in the Open Ocean exhibit and I
lived here—obviously—and we talked every
day through the pipes.

We had *so* much fun. I could tell her the same story over and over again and she'd laugh every time—like it was the first time she'd heard it! Because it *was* like the first time— you know, with her short-term memory thingy.

Anyway, I was heartbroken when she just suddenly disappeared. No good-bye—no nothing. Just silence. So I always wondered what happened—and now she comes back after all this time to find her parents. I mean, how sad is that? Imagine how worried *they've* been. Oh, I've missed her so much.

B Can you keep it down? I'm in bad shape over here. I need my rest to heal.

D This is my tank mate, Bailey. There's *nothing* wrong with him.

B Oh, sure. That's why my head looks like I inhaled a basketball.

D For the hundredth time, all beluga whales have heads that look like yours.

B You don't know what it's like, Destiny. I'm supposed to be able to *echolocate*—to use my head to put out a call and use the echo to find objects far away. But I can't. I *can't*. Stupid head injury. I'm broken!

D Actually, that's not true. I've heard the doctors talking and they say there is nothing wrong with you. You are perfectly healthy.

B I'm clearly very sick.

D Well, at least you can see. Look at me—I can't even see well enough to swim right! Smashing into walls on a daily basis is *not* cool.

B That's nothing. My head definitely feels extra bulbous today. My sinuses must be inflamed!

D (Sigh) Anywaaaay, enough about us.

I'm really worried about Dory! I really hope she can find her parents.

She was excited to learn she was from the Open Ocean exhibit, but got really nervous about the idea of swimming through the pipes to get there because she'd have to go by herself. We're all too big to fit or we'd go with her.

B Hey, I've lost five pounds—stress-induced weight loss. And anyway, grouchy octopus can get her to the Open Ocean exhibit a different way. He's like a magical ninja sorcerer. How does he do that?

D I know. Camouflage is crazy, right?

B Totally crazy. And that's with a missing tentacle. Imagine what he could do if he had all eight! I wish I had a cool skill.

D You *do* have a cool skill, Bailey—echolocation!

B But I *can't!* I am totally messed up. It's all the head damage.

D Oh, Bailey. Remember when you got out of Quarantine? When we first met? (Laughs) I came out of nowhere, right?

B Yes. I remember. And we don't need to talk about it.

D (Laughs) As soon as you noticed me trying to swim by the gate, you were, like—

B I said we don't need to—

D —screaming your head off and shouting, "Ahhhhh! Don't eat me, don't eat me!" Then you passed out! Remember that? (Laughs)

B The end. Ha-ha. So funny.

D Like, how was I going to eat you through a gate? Plus, no teeth. Woulda been kind of tough.

B I had just been through a lot, you know.

D I gave you a minute and then I tried to talk to you again. Remember what you said?

B "Leave me alone?"

D You asked me if I wanted to share some of your dinner.

B No, I didn't.

D Yes, you did. So uncharacteristically sweet.

B My head hurts. I should nap. Can you try and keep it down now?

D (Laughs) Okay, Bailey. And you can have some of *my* dinner later if you'd like.

MARLIN (M) and NEMO (N)

GIFT SHOP, TOY FISH TANK
Marine Life Institute

M It turns out the whole "let a loon take you

where you need to go" thing didn't work.

And now we're . . . here. Trusting a pair of sea lions was my first mistake.

N Yeah, but, Dad—

M Nemo. We were in a pail of water being carried by a loon named Becky. How did I get talked into that? Then Becky hung us in a tree. She hung us in a *tree* so she could get popcorn.

N Dad—

M Then the branch snapped-

N I think because you were moving the pail and—

M The branch snapped and flung us over here into this tank of strange . . . robot fish. And why do they look like Dory?

N I don't know, but—

M Moral of the story? Don't trust sea lions or loons. No . . . you know what the moral of the story is? Don't travel!

N Dad, don't forget that after eating her popcorn, Becky went back to the pail and carried it to Quarantine. We could have been in that pail.

M While that may be true, Nemo, we were not. And so here we are.

N I miss Dory.

M Me too. Somehow, she'd know what to do if she were here. I don't know how she does that.

N I don't think *she* knows, Dad. She just . . . *does.*

M Well, then we'll just have to think . . .

What would Dory do?

HANK

STROLLER
Marine Life Institute courtyard

That's **right**, I'm in a **baby stroller**.

Are you getting a clue about how badly I want out of this institute? I keep telling myself it can't get worse and . . . well, look at me!

I had to make myself look like a baby to trick some nosy human. Do I look like someone who wants to *goo* and *ga*?

I just gotta stay focused on getting that tag and getting to Cleveland. I bet there are no strollers or nosy humans *there*.

That crazy Dory figured we could get across the institute—from the whale tank to the Open Ocean exhibit—by lifting this stroller.

She didn't want to go the most direct way— through the pipes—because she'd have to go alone. The kid clearly doesn't do well with directions, given her whole memory problem. So now I'm stuck taking her the *long* way. We just have to follow the signs to Deep Sea Drive.

And she's swimming inside the sippy cup, telling me which way to go while I do the steering and driving. She's my eyes, so to speak.

It's like wearing a pair of crazy goggles with googly eyes. "Left!" "Right!" "Straight!" Have you ever heard the phrase "the blind leading the blind"? Well, this is more like . . . the nutty leading the very annoyed. I just hope she doesn't get us lost.

Who am I kidding? It's gonna happen, isn't it? Wait a minute—she's taken us off Deep Sea Drive. You got to be kidding me.

What? We are completely off course. No, I don't want to join a cuddle party! What is wrong with this kid? I don't care how cute those fuzzy little otters are. Come on! We gotta go.

Oh, great. Now I've completely lost control of the stroller. Where are we headed now? Oh, no. Nooooooo! (Screams)

STARFISH (S), BURROWING CUCUMBER (C), ANEMONE (A), SEA WORM (W)

TOUCH POOL
Marine Life Institute

If you're living in the **touch** pool, you're living in fear.

Squeezed!

You're grabbed, poked, **prodded**—

Pinched!

A Snatched up out of the tank and stared at real close . . . It's like they're thinking about breaking you open to see your insides.

S I had some kids turn me into a triangle once!

C Once, I got stretched so hard my midsection never snapped back. That's why I have these rolls. Really, we endure all kinds of torture here.

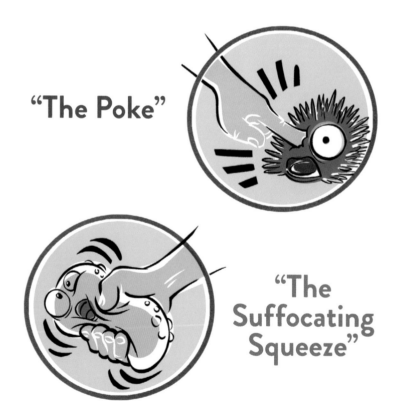

"The Poke"

"The Suffocating Squeeze"

"The Scramble"

"The Taffy Pull"

"The Dangler"

S It's an absolute nightmare. But today . . . today was a day to go down in the history books.

A Sing it, sister.

W Best day ever!

S This blue tang and an octopus somehow ended up in the touch tank. Which was very weird—that's never happened before.

C And they kept saying, "Just keep swimming," chanting it over and over again.

W Wise words!

C Very wise.

A I heard someone say they were trying to get to the Open Ocean exhibit.

S Huh. Interesting.

Anyway, once they released the hands, it was business as usual. I had a kid lift me out and he and his friends started putting me in a Taffy Pull. They were each pulling an arm in separate directions.

C It's like they don't know you're a living, breathing thing!

A I was in a combo lock: the Scramble and the Suffocating Squeeze.

W We were in a group Dangler!

S Then one of the hands poked the octopus so hard that it made him ink! It was incredible! A cloud of black came over the tank.

A It was beautiful!

W Glorious!

C It was genius!

S That octopus—he's a real hero.

A The Great Pink One!

W Oooh, Great Pink One!

S They had to close the tank to clean it, so all the hands left. We had peace! We had freedom! We had a party!

A We made this monument in the Great Pink One's honor.

S But we don't know what happened to him and his blue tang friend. They just disappeared. Almost like . . . did they really exist? But of course they did!

We got our day!

The Great Pink One will live in our fondest memories forever, as our hero. And the wise words of him and his friend will be chanted throughout the walls of this tank for eternity.

Just keep swimming!

LOUDMOUTH CLAM

OUTDOOR TIDAL POOL EXHIBIT
Marine Life Institute

Oh. Well, hello there, my friend.

Boy, it feels good to talk. I love a good conversation. Oh, who am I kidding? I love every conversation—even the bad ones are great.

Why, I had a lovely conversation just a little bit ago with a couple of clownfish who stopped by. What a surprise that was. Haven't seen anyone come around here in a long time. They were a friendly pair, though, so that was nice. Father and son—looked the part, too. You could tell they were related.

Anyway, they kept talking about someone named Dory—Dory this and Dory that. But I'd never heard of her. They said they've traveled all over the institute trying to find her, swimming from a tank in the gift shop, then flopping toward the plaza fountain, which propelled them into my tidal pool exhibit. And now they're headed through the pipes to Quarantine. What great lengths they have gone to to find this Dory!

I'll tell you what, though: if she's anything like Shelley, those two are better off without her! I hope they don't find her. She'll only break their happy little clownfish hearts.

Shelley . . . why, Shelley, *why*? Why, why, why? That scallop broke my heart with her feminine wiles and those beautiful eyes . . . all one hundred of 'em. Gorgeous!

Ah, Shelley . . . We ate plankton together, went on short strolls . . . you know, as much as we could. But it didn't matter that we didn't get very far. We had deep conversations as we burrowed into the sand. We even wrote each other love poems.

I can still remember the last poem I wrote for her: Shelley, Shelley, oh, be true. Shelley, Shelley, (cries) I . . . (cries) love . . . you (cries).

I loved you so much and . . . you turned my heart to poo! (Cries hysterically)

Well, that last part I just made up right now.

That wasn't part of the original poem.

You see, she took off with a mussel. A mussel! You believe that?

When I think about it, I still can't believe she's really gone. Oh, Shelley. How could you be so coldhearted? I would never have expected it to end the way it did! Why, oh, why?

And yet . . . maybe if I'd gone to great lengths to find her, like those clownfish swimming all over the institute to find their friend, we'd be together now.

Ohhh, Shelleyyyyyyyyyyy! I'm sorry! Come back, Shelleyyyyyyyyyyyyyyyy!

BILL (B) and CAROL (C)

OPEN OCEAN EXHIBIT
Marine Life Institute

We've lived here for—**well**, as long as I can remember, so we know the area **well**. Right, Bill?

Yeah. **We live here**, Carol.

C And today we met this strange little blue tang. I noticed her right away, because all the other blue tangs were gone. They all went to

Quarantine. But she didn't even have a tag. She seemed very confused.

B Why are you talking about this, Carol? You should mind your own business.

C Oh, hush. He thinks I'm too friendly. And you know what? Margaret saw something earlier.

B Oh, no, not Margaret!

C Yes, Margaret. She's my best friend.

B You know you stir up trouble when you mess in other people's business. Remember what happened with the Allens.

C Oh, Bill. Really—

B Really. If it weren't for you meddling, I'd still be invited to poker night.

C Oh, Bill.

B It's true.

C I heard they're not even doing poker night anymore.

B So you *ruined it for everybody*!

C I didn't ruin anything. Can I finish telling the story? So Margaret was out searching for sand dollars like she does every afternoon, just—

B Ha! Yeah, right. You mean searching to feed the gossip machine!

C Just minding her own business when she saw a seven-armed octopus—

B That would make him a septopus—

C Uh-huh. She saw a septopus bring the blue tang here. He carried her clear across the room over to the tank! Can you imagine?

Then the blue tang *gave* the septopus her tag, and he dropped her into the tank and left! What does it all mean?

B You just keep on going. You can't stop. Can you, Carol?

C Anyway, I could tell something was wrong with that blue tang right away, and naturally I tried to help. When we told her that all the other blue tangs had just gone to Quarantine to wait for their truck to Cleveland, she got very upset, didn't she, Bill?

B Yeah. Sure.

C I told her she could easily get to Quarantine. You just go through the pipes. But she said she would get lost—said she couldn't remember things. And really, it couldn't be simpler—two lefts and a right.

B (Eye roll)

C She kept saying she was afraid she'd forget. Now that's strange, right? Anyway, she took off and went into the pipes. I do hope she managed to find her way.

B Maybe you should go look for her.

C Oh, Bill. Just remember: if I wasn't friendly, we'd have never met, because you never talk to anyone. You've always been that way. Just like to keep to yourself.

B That's true.

C So just imagine. If it weren't for my friendly nature, you might be here cutting the grass, all alone. And that would be very sad.

B Would it, though? Kidding. She's actually right. I don't like it too quiet.

C See? He's all sweet and gooey under that hard shell. The grass looks very nice, by the way, honey. You should take a break.

B Okay. And . . . guess what? I got something for us to share.

C *Blue algae?* My favorite. You rascal.

B Scraped it off your favorite rock.

C Bill. Thank you.

B (Smiles)

DORY

PIPES LEADING TO QUARANTINE
Marine Life Institute

Everything's **okay** now.

Everything's okay. I was alone—here in the pipes—and completely lost. I couldn't remember the directions and then I started getting really scared, because, well, you see, I don't always remember things so well. I get lost pretty easily.

But then I did remember something . . . *pipes*—
pipe pals! Destiny! So I called to Destiny
through the pipes in whale. Like this:

DeeeeeSTINYYYYYYYYY!

And she heard me! She answered back! I
told her I was lost and she said she would
try and help. Then she convinced Bob—no,
that's not it. . . . Was it Jacob? No. Um . . .
Billy? Well, doesn't matter—she convinced
her beluga whale tank mate to try using
his echolocation to find me. He went all
OoooooooooOOOOOooo and it
worked! It really *worked*! He didn't think he
could do it, but then . . . he could! Because
he tried. He just needed to believe in himself!
How great is that? I feel like there's a good
lesson in there somewhere.

It's probably that I should try echolocating,
too. **OoooooooOOOOoo00.** Nope.
Doesn't work for me.

I believe I can do it.

OooooooOOOOoooo.

Nope. Still not working. Too bad. I'll practice. Anyway, he used his echolocation and Destiny told me which way to go. They worked together and guided me through the pipes!

Then something funny happened. Bailey and Destiny—THAT'S HIS NAME! BAILEY! Anyway, Whaley and Destiny could tell there was someone coming toward me. And guess who it was. Marlin and Nemo!

I heard Destiny calling my name, so I called back to her and told her **I FOUND MAAAAAAaaaRLIN anNNND NeeeEEEmmmMOOOO!**

And—here's the best part—do you know what Marlin said? He told me that he and Nemo were stuck and didn't know what to do until they thought, *What would Dory do?* And that got them all the way from the gift shop (I wish I would've known they were there; I would've loved to pick up something for my parents) to er . . . a tank with a sad ram (or was it someone named Sam?) . . . to here! *What would Dory do?* Can you believe that? Even just repeating it makes my scales all bumpy—look. They actually thought about what I would do in order to figure it out! And it worked. The "What-would-Dory-do" question helped them find me!

I think maybe I'll try that when I get in a pickle—and it'll be easy because I am Dory. Right? So I just have to ask, "What would I do?" That is so cool! Wait. What am I doing? Oh, yeah. I'm doing what I do. I'm Dory . . . just doing what I do. What would Dory do? A fin flip. A spin. A roller-coaster twirl. Okay. Did it.

So anyway, now Marlin, Nemo, and I are going to meet my parents in the Guillotine.

No. That's not right. The Creamery? Ugh.
No . . . Quarantine! Quarantine! And I'm
leading the way because, well, what would
Dory do? She'd lead the way! And she
wouldn't be afraid about going places alone
anymore. Dory would just do what Dory does.

I can't believe I am about to meet my parents.
I am so excited. And a little nervous. I hope
they remember me . . . and I remember them.

BLUE TANGS
1 (①), 2 (②), 3 (③)

BLUE TANG TANK ON TRANSPORT TRUCK
Outside Quarantine, Marine Life Institute

Well, **all of us** here are loaded up in the truck. . . .

We're all excited for Cleveland.

Not *everyone*.

1 *Most* of us are excited. I've never ridden in a truck before. And Cleveland should be nice. I think we're leaving soon, but we're all still in such a tizzy over the news. It's all we can talk about.

3 I just can't believe it's true: Dory actually came back. After all these years she came back!

2 I wouldn't have believed it if I didn't see it for myself. She was always so forgetful. Could hardly remember her own name!

1 It was nice to see that she had a little help— two nice clownfish and a grouchy octopus. I think he was missing a tentacle? Anyway, they helped her find her way here. She was looking for Jenny and Charlie.

3 It was just awful telling her the news. I could barely look at her. She had come all this way . . . only to find out—they're gone.

What daughter wants to hear that?

1 Jenny and Charlie would have been so proud.
They loved her so much. It's just about the
saddest thing ever. The poor thing. It breaks
my heart.

3 I know. And she was so upset. Upset and
then . . . I can't even think about it.

1 Terrible. After we told Dory her parents were
gone, she . . . fell onto the floor and slipped
right down the drain in Quarantine!

2 That drain goes straight out to the ocean.
Can't imagine she'll be able to find her way
alone down there. Not with her memory
problem and all.

1 The nice clownfish and octopus are still here.
They're upset, trying to figure out a way to
help her. They are clearly very good friends.
But . . . I don't know how they'd possibly make

their way out of here. The humans loaded them onto the truck with the rest of us, didn't even check them for tags.

3 I guess it's off to Cleveland for all of us. I hope she's okay.

2 Me too.

DORY

OCEAN
Outside Marine Life Institute

I'm **alone** and **scared** and I'm **all alone.**

Completely alone. I lost everyone. Marlin and Nemo . . . my parents. They're gone. They're gone! I finally made it to Quarantine—to the blue tang tank and . . . they told me my parents are gone. I feel like I can't breathe. It's like my insides were all jumbled up and then put back the wrong way and—and now it's like I can't breathe right.

Hello? I'm lost. After the other blue tangs told me about my parents, I fell down the drain and through the pipes and out here into the ocean! And now I'm all alone and what am I supposed to do? They were supposed to be there and they weren't. And now I've lost Marlin and Nemo and everyone and . . . I don't know what to do.

What should I do? What can I do? What would . . . what would Lori do? Wait—what would *Dory* do? Right! *What would I do?* Okay. Let me just look around and see . . . if I look over there and over here . . . maybe I can find something to help if I just keep swimming and looking . . . there. Kelp. I know kelp. Kelp is better. Okay. And there's sand. I love sand.

It's soft and squishy. And there's a rock . . .
and, oh, look. Shells! I love shells.

They're all lined up, sorta like a path. . . . That
seems sorta familiar. Oooh, look! That one
looks like a pineapple. Shell, shell, shell,
shell . . . There's a taco. That one looks like a

cloud. Ooh. That's a nice one. I like that one.
I'll just go this way and follow the shells. . . .
We're winding that way and . . . let's see where
it leads. . . .

JENNY (J) and CHARLIE (C)

OCEAN
Outside Marine Life Institute

J Our Dory is back! We're all together again.
Oh, we've waited so long for this day.

C She found us out here in the ocean! Our kelpcake found us!

J I'm so happy, Charlie.

C I know, sweetheart. So am I.

J Of course, I feel terrible about the way she blamed herself, though. Oh, it was just awful. She was apologizing for forgetting and getting lost. . . . It was just so upsetting to see her like that.

C I know. But you said it best, sweetheart. You reminded her that she was the one who found us! *She* found *us*. Dory did that.

J That's right. She did.

C See, we figured she'd gone through the pipes into the ocean, so we set out shells all around.

J Trails of shells, out in every direction—leading to us.

C We used to do it when she was little and—

J She remembered! She remembered and she followed those shells, just like we taught her.

C She remembered.

J And she's so grown-up now. I'm so proud of her.

C Me too.

J We have missed her so much.

All this time I kept thinking about her sweet little face and imagining what she would look like all grown-up. Oh, Charlie. Do you remember the day she was born? With those big, beautiful eyes . . .

C That, I do remember. I don't remember much else from that day. I was a bundle of nerves. I thought I was all ready and then when it was time, I was like a whirlpool—swimming around and around and around—

J (Laughs) Yes, yes. You were just so excited and happy. Ohhh, remember how she reached out and touched my fin?

C And then she touched me with the other. I think we melted right down into the sand. Like a pair of burrowing cucumbers.

J And now . . . now she's all grown-up. (Sniffles) Oh, I'm sorry. I'm still a little emotional about the whole thing.

C It's okay, sweetheart. It's okay. But you know what? You don't have to be sad anymore. Because she's back.

J You're right, Charlie. She is back with us.

C And all this time we were worried that Dory would be alone—you know, that she'd have a hard time making friends. And it turns out she's got great friends.

J They do sound very nice.

C Two clownfish named . . . Marlin and Nemo. And Dory is determined to help them. See, last she saw them, they were about to be loaded into a truck at the institute.

J I'm a little nervous about it. I don't know how—

C No, no. Remember? We don't need to know how, because Dory does.

J I know, I know. She has a plan and she's so determined. She gets that from you, sweetheart.

C Well, she has your resourcefulness.

J Ohhh. Thanks, honey. She does come up with a lot of ideas.

C And it doesn't take her more than a minute. I mean, she thought about Marlin and Nemo stuck on that truck and suddenly—*POP!* Lightbulb. She had an idea.

J (Laughs) That's right. And she called on some other friends to help.

C She's got so many friends!

J One of them is a whale.

C She's talking to her right now. Her whale-speaking is amazing, by the way.

J (Laughs) I know. She's so talented, isn't she? With my eyes closed, I'd think she was a whale!

C That's right. (Eyes closed) Wait. What's that I hear? There's a whale coming this way. (Laughs) She's incredible. And we're never going to lose her again.

DESTINY (**D**) and BAILEY (**B**)

WHALE TANK
Marine Life Institute

D I can't!

B You can.

D I—

B It's for Dory! She needs us.

D I know. Of course I want to help Dory, but . . . Ahhhh! I won't make it out there in the ocean! I CAN'T SEE! How can I swim if I can't see?!

B Snap out of it, Destiny!

D (Screams)

B Look at me. Look at my bulbous head. I used to think this bulbous head was defective. And it was. Because you know what? I thought I couldn't do something that I could do. I didn't know that bulbous is *beautiful*. And full of powers that don't even make sense! And who taught me that? You.

D But—

B Shhhhh, shhhhhhh. You helped me find my inner bulbous beauty. And so . . . I shall be your eyes.

D What?

B I'll be your eyes. I'll guide you. Tell you which way to go.

D But the walls . . . so many walls! They're everywhere and I can't see them and what if—

B There are no walls in the ocean.

D No walls? Seriously? None?

B It's your destiny, Destiny.

D Let's do this thing! For Dory.

B Yes! For Dory! Now . . . jump! One, two . . . Wait, careful! *That's* a wall!

D AHHHHHHHHH!

B AHHHHHHHHH!

FLUKE (F) and RUDDER (R) (and GERALD (G))

CLUSTER OF ROCKS
Morro Bay, outside Marine Life Institute

This **better** be worth moving for, mate.

F I know. But I think it just might be. You don't see something like this every day. Whales and blue tangs on some sort of mission.

R True, true.

F Bizarre, it is. What do you think they're doing exactly?

R I think they might be trying to stop that truck.

F Off their rockers, all of them. The two whales jumped out of their tank—at the institute— right into the ocean.

R That's right. Then the one with the puffy head started doing something weird with his mouth. He was going, "OoooOOoooOOoooo."

F Echolocating, he was.

R Right, right. Next thing you know, the whales are leading the way to the bridge, following the truck. It's exhausting just watching 'em. (Yawn)

F I know. (Yawn) Maybe we should head back to our—hey! Gerald!

G (Giggles)

F For crying out loud, Gerald! Get off the rock! The nerve!

R Oy! Get off the rock, Gerald! Don't get used to it!

G (Giggles)

DORY

BRIDGE
Freeway outside Marine Life Institute

ThhhhhaaaanNNNK YyyYYyyoooOOuuUUU, DeeeEEsSSsstinnnNNny!

That was great. Destiny and Bailey were such a help. Good to have friends, right? Especially when you're trying to save a couple of other friends from a truck headed to Sweden! Well, that doesn't sound right. Hmmm . . . Oh yeah, a truck headed to *Cleveland*.

And you know what I realized? Marlin and Nemo? They're more than friends. They're family. Just like my parents—and did I tell you I found them? I did! And they're just like I remembered. They're cute and funny and great and—oh! Wait. What was I doing? Saving Marlin and Nemo? Right!

Bailey did his whole "OooooooooOOOooOOooO" thing and found the truck! It was driving away and heading straight for the bridge! So I had to think . . . What would Dory do? What *would* Dory do . . . ?

Well, then I saw a bunch of adorable otters—I mean, look at these guys. You wanna just squeeze them, right? Have you ever seen anything so cute? They're just these little fuzzy wuzzy squishy cutie pies I want to hug!

So anyway, they gave me an idea. Hmm . . .
What was it again? What would Dory do,
what would Dory do? Right! Cuddle party!
These guys are SO cute they'll be able to stop
traffic—and that's what we're going to do.
We need to stop traffic and stop that truck.

So the otters climbed up onto each other
to get to the bridge and then Destiny used
her tail to flip me aaaaaaall the way to the
otters. Which, I have to admit, was pretty fun.
Like flying! My parents didn't want me to go,
because they were afraid of losing me again.
Isn't that sweet? They were worried I might
forget. But I told them if it happened . . . and
it probably won't, but *if* it did . . . I would find
them again. Because I would. But we have
something important happening right now.
Right now isn't about me finding anyone, it's
about . . . cute otters . . . cuddling! Cuddle
party time, everyone! Awwwwwww. How cute
is this? They just love to cuddle.

Yes! It's working! (Gasp) The cars are stopping! People are taking pictures. Whew! I've been out here for a while now. Kinda hard to breathe out here in the air, huh? (Gasp) Smile for the cameras, everyone. (Gasp) Um . . . anyone else seeing these floating green and pink polka-dot things? So bright and flashy. You know . . . I think . . . cute otters, you . . . take me to truck? Yes? Fast . . . please . . . thanks . . . wuzzy.

MARLIN (Ⓜ) and NEMO (Ⓝ)

BLUE TANG TANK ON TRANSPORT TRUCK
Freeway outside Marine Life Institute

> So **Dory's** here now.

Ⓝ She had a whale flip her up to the bridge and started an otter cuddle party to stop all the cars! Then the otters helped her get to the truck! How cool is that? I wish I got to do it!

M Well, it wasn't very safe–right? I'm sure many injuries have happened that very same way.

N But she made it. And she's totally fine!

M Yeah, that's right. Dory made it here, onto the truck. Hank grabbed her and put her into a tank.

N She came all the way over here because she couldn't leave us. She said she couldn't leave her *family* behind. We're her family, too!

M That's right. That's our Dory. Only now we're *all* stuck on the truck. Dory, me, and Nemo–

N But Dory will get us out of here, Dad. I just know she will.

M Or . . . you know what? Maybe *I* can get us off the truck.

N How?

M Coooo cooo loooo loooo . . .

N Great idea, Dad! Call Becky!

M Here she comes!

BECKY

OCEAN
Outside Marine Life Institute

Squawk! Squawk! Squawk!

Squawk! Squawk! Squawk!

Cooo-ooooo-ooooo. Oo-roooo. Oooo-rooo.
Cooo-ooooo-ooooo. Oo-roooo.
Oooo-rooo loooo.

Squawk! Squawk! Squawk!

Squawk! Squawk! Squawk!

Looo loo loo loo. Oooo-rooo.
Cooo-ooooo-ooooo. Oo-roooo. Oooo-rooo.

SquawwwwwkKKKKKKKkkkkkkkkk!!!!!!!!!

SPLASH!

Squawk! Squawk! Squawk!

Cooo-ooooo-ooooo. Oo-roooo. Oooo-rooo.
Squawk! Squawk! Oooo-rooo.

SLAM!

Squawk! Squawk! Squawk!

Editor's translation:

Oh, trusty pail, we fly once more
Another mission, as before.
Two fish we carry in our glory.
Why are they screaming?
Who is this "Dory"?

Okay, little clownfish, if you say so, I shall
Return you to the sea, then back I go.

SPLASH!

I fly and I fly to continue my quest.

For this weary loon, there is no rest.

Here at the truck, I return once more.

Peer in with lonely eyes . . .

Who am I looking for?

Oh! The fish called "Dory,"

Like a symphony!

She is giving a seven-armed grouch

Quite a soliloquy.

Creeeeeeeek. BAM!

SLAM!

Ohhhhh, NOOOOooo! The door slammed!

All of us—of scale and feather,

Locked inside—oh, how to weather?

No sky to see! Four walls! A ceiling!

How can I explain this feeling?

My chest as shallow as a bowl.

Dizzy!

Dazed!

My mind, a spring roll.

Soy sauce, tofu, eggs, and rice,

Vegetables, noodles, scrambled twice.

Release! Release! A powerful word!

Release! Release!

Hear this lonely jailbird!

Release! Release!

The fish chant loud and clear.

Release! Release!

Will no one hear?

Trapped inside a room on wheels,

Short of

Breath,

Weak

In

The

Heels,

The loon is going down, my friends.
A mere fainting spell–this shan't
Be the end!

When the doors reopen,
Wake me for my refrain!
And Rebecca shall soar once again!

HANK

INSIDE TRANSPORT TRUCK
Freeway outside Marine Life Institute

I guess you're probably wondering **why** I'm driving a truck.

It's nuts, I know. But how else are we gonna get back to the ocean? That's right. I'm not going to Cleveland. I'm going back to the ocean. I'm surprised, too. I never would have guessed I'd be saying that. But here I am. And you know why? Dory. It's all because of her. Apparently, losing a tentacle isn't the only way to change an octopus. She made me realize it's nice to have certain folks around—especially good-hearted ones like her.

So back to the truck-driving thing. It went like this. They had us locked up in the back of the truck—along with that crazy-looking loon bird, by the way. Anyway, we start moving—on our way to Cleveland. I'm figuring there's no way outta this. We're done. But then Dory—always with the "there's always a way" thing. The kid's incredible. And she was right. There actually *was* a way. We spotted this hatch up in the roof of the truck.

So Dory and I—we climbed out. Then—and here's my favorite part—I splatted myself right across the windshield! If you could have seen the look on those dopey humans' faces. I tell you, I've never had so much fun in all my life! Scared the chowder out of them! It was hilarious.

So anyway, naturally, the dopes stop the truck and jump out to see what the heck is on their windshield. They jump out and we go in. I lock the doors and put Dory in the cup of water inside the cup holder. I'm in the driver's seat and we're ready to rock. Dory and I figure out how to maneuver the truck. Pretty simple, really. Throw it into gear . . . steer the wheel. Piece of cake.

We take off, leaving those dopey humans looking like a pair of blowfish—standing there, looking totally shocked and clueless. It was a-mazing.

So Dory's watching the road and navigating from the cup—just like we did with the stroller. She shouts directions and I drive. She's telling me to go left and we're going around and around . . . in a circle, it turns out.

Hey, first time behind the wheel, okay? Cut me a break. Anyway, we nearly smash into those dopey drivers!

Then—get this—we're going the wrong way. Cars are swerving, horns are honking . . . total chaos.

Dory sees a car pulling a boat and decides we should follow it. But when we get closer to the guy, she sees he's sunburned and has got sand all over his feet! Probably just *leaving* the ocean. So we turn around. And now we're heading in the opposite direction. I'm not worried at all. We'll get there.

Wait a minute. Oh, no. You gotta be kidding me. Hang on. We're running out of gas! We're on fumes! We better hurry!
What the—

If I'm not mistaken that is the poop of seagulls—aka, flying sea rats. Well, guess what, pals? You're gonna lead us straight to the sea, thank you very much.

WHOOOP! WHOOOP!

Oh, great. It's the fuzz. Hang on—I mean it this time!

OFFICER DAVE

FREEWAY
Outside Marine Life Institute

Well, my partner and I were on **traffic** detail.

Around 7:26 a.m. the perps, described by witnesses as a seven-legged octopus—er, septopus—and a blue tang fish, drove by in a stolen vehicle from the Marine Life Institute near exit seventeen. We immediately began pursuit. The perps, whoever they were, drove recklessly, making circles, nearly hitting a couple of pedestrians, who, my sources inform me, were the original drivers of the stolen vehicle. The drivers were uninjured but "weirded out." One was also quoted as saying he was "so fired" and "bummed" because he'd "have to move into Grammy's basement again."

After that, the perps were going opposite the flow of traffic, causing mass confusion and major traffic delays. No serious injuries have been reported. As my partner and I continued pursuit, they abruptly changed direction after a flock of seagulls passed overhead. At that point, the vehicle began heading toward the ocean. The truck continued picking up speed, and at approximately 7:34 it drove off the bridge and into the Pacific Ocean.

The perps committed a number of offenses and crimes, which I have listed here in my report.

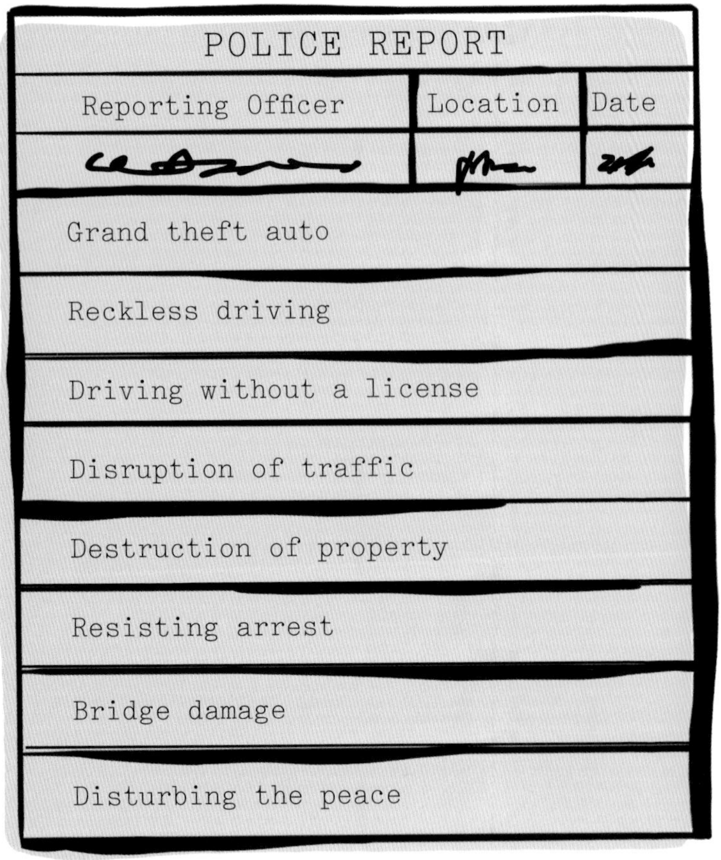

POLICE REPORT		
Reporting Officer	Location	Date
[illegible]	[illegible]	[illegible]
Grand theft auto		
Reckless driving		
Driving without a license		
Disruption of traffic		
Destruction of property		
Resisting arrest		
Bridge damage		
Disturbing the peace		

I believe it was an inside job. Premeditated. The truck left the institute, got onto the freeway, and soon headed toward the ocean. What were these criminals playing at? I suppose at this point we can only guess. They're in the ocean now, so we'll never catch 'em.

DORY (Ⓓ) (and MARLIN (Ⓜ), HANK (Ⓗ), NEMO (Ⓝ), BAILEY (Ⓑ), CHARLIE (Ⓒ), JENNY (Ⓙ), and DESTINY (Ⓓ), too!)

HOME
Great Barrier Reef

Can you **believe** it?

We made it back to the reef—everybody.
We're all here, together, back home on the
reef. Even Destiny and Bailey! They decided
to come live with us! And with Bailey's help,
Destiny is swimming like a pro! She's not

afraid of smashing into things anymore. Between that and her awesome tail-flipping skills, the little ones are always asking her for rides. I am so happy. I'm as happy as a clam. Though from what Marlin and Nemo said, clams can be pretty glum. Maybe it's "I'm as happy as Spam"?

Oh, hello! I am so happy to be home. And do you know what the icing on the kelpcake is? (Laughs) I know—my dad still calls me that. It's kinda sweet. Ohhh, I could really go for a kelpcake right now. Or a churro . . . What were we talking about again?

Anyway, I'm not afraid to go off on my own anymore. I can swim alone, check things out. I can swim all the way over to that weird squishy thing. . . .

See? Or I can swim all the way over here . . . just see what I see. . . . Oh, hello, little chunk of slime. Go over here . . .

What's up, piece-o'-seaweed-far-from-my-home? See? Swimming around all by myself. I'm cool. No worries. No fear of getting lost . . . Life is just amazingly wonderful.

M All right, everybody! Family swim leaves in five minutes. We gotta make sure we get back before it gets dark!

H You're screaming in my face. I'm right here. I'm ready.

M Ah! Sorry. Didn't see you there, Hank.

N I'm the leader today! Bailey, help me find a really cool cave.

B Of course. Let me just turn on my navi. OoooOOOOOOooooooOOOOooooo.

C Kelpcake!

J Dory, we're getting ready to go!

(D) DooooooorrrrrRRRRR rrryYYYYYYYYy, FfffaaaaammmMMMMM mmmmmIlLLLLLLy SwwWWWWWWWiiiiiIIIMM mmmmmm.

(D) I'MMMMmmmmmm CooOOOOmmMMMMm IIIIIliiiiNNNnnNNnnNG, DeeeEEsSSsstinnnNNny.

I gotta get going. Family swim. It's kinda funny, right? I left looking for my parents and realized that I had a family here, too, with Nemo and Marlin.

And now I have an even bigger family. Hank, Bailey, Destiny . . . we're all here together. And what could be better than that?

The en—wait.
What were we
talking about?